FURY OF FATE

COREENE CALLAHAN

OLIVER
HEBER
BOOKS

To the brave ones. May you always be so courageous.

L ove hurt. Evidence of it stood across the street. One hundred feet, two raised voices, and a shitload of annoyance away. Gaze riveted to the couple, Ivar slid deeper into the shadows, and using the narrow alleyway for cover, settled in to watch the show. Listen to it, too. His favorite companion, a bottle of Jim Beam, dangling from his fingertips, he rotated his wrist. Whiskey sloshed against glass, joining the whisper of winter wind as he shook his head.

Jesus. Humans and their drama.

It never ended. Witness the fact the female staged the scene in a public place. Right out in the open. Drawing sidelong glances from passersby on a sidewalk in city central. Cheeks flushed, she pointed a slender finger at her companion, accusing him of cheating, telling him this time was the last straw, refusing to take it anymore. Ivar snorted. Right. *The last straw*. A likely story. Nothing but a big fat lie.

He could tell by the way she held herself—shoulders hunched beneath her expensive coat instead of squared. Tears in her eyes instead of steely determination. Gloved hand shaking instead of rock steady. Ivar sighed and took another swig of J.B. Beyond disappointing. She should be walking away from the dumbass, but...nah. Her body language was all wrong, 100 percent non-assertive. The raw hitch in her voice, though, was the true tip-off. A real fuck-you to feminism, telling Ivar all he needed to know. The human male had nothing to worry about. His lady love wasn't going anywhere. She lacked the ingredients required when threatening to leave another.

Backbone. Bravery. The courage to go it alone.

Tightening his grip on his buddy in a bottle, Ivar swallowed another mouthful. The whiskey went down smooth. The burn of discontent circling the inside of his chest, however—not so much. Just like the female across the street, he ached with it. Hurt deep down where old wounds festered and new ones never healed. Stifling a snarl, Ivar propped his shoulder against the brick building façade. His eyes narrowed on the squabbling couple. He really should oust the pair.

Unlock the chains, release his dragon half and...

Send the lovebirds running for their lives.

No doubt the smart thing to do. He didn't, after all, have much time. Too bad compelling the duo with magic—and his special brand of mind control—held little appeal. Odd in more ways than one. Out of character for him too. As a general rule, he enjoyed scaring the hell out of humans. Razing the inferior race equaled big fun. At least, most nights. Tonight, though, didn't qualify as *most*. He was tired. So goddamn sick of everyone and everything. Which meant he needed to cross the street and get on with it. Do what he'd flown into Seattle to accomplish. But as he listened to the escalating argument, Ivar couldn't make himself move.

Emotional gridlock. Physical lockdown. Mental anguish.

All were present tonight, keeping his feet glued to cracked pavement. Which left him neck deep in the kind of turmoil he didn't normally experience, never mind know what to do with. Emotion wasn't his forte. Until recently, he'd thought himself incapable of feeling anything. Untouchable. Numbed out. Beyond help. A state of grace Ivar knew no longer applied to him. And hadn't for months. The death of his best friend had seen to that, cracking him wide open. Now he bled sorrow, grieving in ways he didn't understand and couldn't shut down.

Picking at the frayed corner of the bottle label, Ivar frowned. He needed it to stop. Wanted the numbness to return and the hurt to go away. No doubt a childish wish. Life wasn't simple. Neither was mourning a friend, so...fuck it. Guess pain and suffering was par for the course and his for the duration. Which—yeah —made him want to hammer the humans even more. His gaze ping-ponged between the male and female. Jesus help him, but the twits deserved it—for causing a scene, for contributing to noise pollution, for being part of the problem instead of the solution. One that began with environmental crisis and ended with the death of the planet along with every living creature on Earth.

Pure selfishness. Abhorrent greed. So incredibly short-sighted.

The human race owned it all in spades.

But worse? None of them gave a damn about cause and effect. Or the fact the planet they called home died a little more each day. The *cause* was easy to pin-point...the human race. The *effect* was more cat-astrophic. Environmental meltdown on a massive scale. Proof of it headlined the news every evening—monster storms, record setting temperatures, shrinking polar icecaps, the rise of disease and...

Shit. He could go on...and on.

And on.

He shut it down instead. Whining wouldn't solve the problem. Taking the imbeciles across the street out, however, just might. Gaze narrowed on the lovebirds, Ivar flexed his hand. Magic bloomed. Pink flame licked across the center of his palm. Hmm yeah, that felt unbelievable...like power, glory, and the promise of something better. Something shiny and bright. Something more than the relentless despair circling behind his breastbone. Inhaling deep, Ivar filled his lungs, then exhaled smooth. The chill took up the cause, sending his breath out in a stream of frosty air. God, it would be so easy to kill the pair. A soft murmur. A rudimentary spell. A little Dragonkind hocus-pocus, and a fireball would rise upon command. Nothing left to do then but wind up and let the inferno fly.

Slam-bang. Sizzle, burn, scream...poof-gone.

Nothing but two piles of human ash on the sidewalk with a minimal amount of trouble. Ivar swirled the whiskey in the bottle and pursed his lips. Tempting...oh so very *tempting*, but not nearly satisfying enough. KOing a couple of humans wouldn't alleviate the tension, never mind assuage the source of his aggravation. His frustration stemmed from a much larger problem. He needed to get his act together and his ass in gear. Before he ran out of time and his warriors came looking for him.

Not an optimal outcome.

He didn't want any interference right now. Tonight belonged to him. Not to the humans and global issues.

Not to the warriors under his command or the greater health of the Razorback organization. Just him. Only him. He hadn't snuck out of the lair, slipped past his personal guards, and flown downtown to become distracted from his larger goal. Or get caught in the middle of a domestic dispute. The melodrama unfolding across the street wasn't his concern. Here and now didn't have a thing to do with a couple of squabbling humans. It did, however, have everything to do with him.

He needed to be alone. To mourn his loss and honor the dead.

Brows drawn tight, Ivar fisted his hand, snuffing out magical flame in favor of getting back on track. Pushing away from the brick wall, he stepped out of the shadows and onto the sidewalk. Half-frozen puddles cracked beneath his boots. Sharp sound traveled, rolling down the narrow avenue. Despair welled, collecting behind his breastbone. Fighting the rising tide, Ivar stared at the building he still owned. So much damage. Not much left to salvage. Little wonder. The fire had shown no mercy, licking through shattered windows to blacken the face of pale stone. Now the roof sagged, and the once beautiful brownstone looked sad. Beyond hope beneath the gloom of midnight and the weak light thrown by nearby lampposts.

Deuces...a once thriving nightclub in the center of Seattle.

Now nothing but a burned out shell.

Disastrous destruction, courtesy of the war Ivar fought with the Nightfury pack—a group of Dragonkind warriors who didn't agree with his politics. Or the plan he put in place to solve the environmental problems plaguing the planet. To be expected, he guessed. He knew Bastian—commander of the Nightfury pack—better than most. Had trained with the male, coming up in the same dragon combat training squadron in Europe. Once brothers-in-arms, now forever enemies. The finality of it should've bothered him. It had—years ago—but not anymore. Fate was fickle, spinning a male with a flick of her fingers, sending warriors down different paths and...

Sometimes on a collision course with one another.

Win some. Lose some.

Just like three nights ago. One building destroyed. Five Razorback warriors dead. And the entire reason he was here, revisiting a place he'd once considered his home away from home. With a sigh, Ivar stepped off the curb. Pace steady and strides smooth, he crossed the street. Startled by the sound of his footfalls, the couple glanced his way. Both flinched. The female met his gaze. Hers widened in appreciation an instant before fear spiked in her scent.

Same old, same old.

Women always reacted to him that way. Fascination and arousal first. Alarm and a healthy dose of wariness second. Some overcame the second in favor of the first, bypassing smart in favor of stupid, wanting to try him on for size. Not that Ivar liked to brag, but...yeah. He knew his appeal and always delivered. Sex, after all, equaled the best of all things—relaxation in the form of release. So instead of snarling at her, he winked, and slipping between two parked cars, waited. If he got lucky the bastard would take offense and enter the ring to defend his lady love. Fortune, after all, favored the—

The bastard spun on his heel. Snagging the female's arm, and with a muttered "come on, Sally," the coward hightailed it toward the intersection at the other end of the street. Heavy footfalls along with the clatter of high heels shattered the quiet.

Ivar rolled his eyes, and dragging his gaze from the fleeing couple, mounted Deuce's front steps. Three treads from the top, he unleashed his magic. Wood groaned. The plywood boarding up the entrance shattered, blowing into the marble-clad entryway. Splinters hammered the back wall, then fell to the floor, joining the smear of ash and soot on the mosaic tiles. The scent of smoke still hung in the air, gathering like wispy ghouls against the high ceiling. Without a moment's hesitation, Ivar stepped over the threshold and...

Into chaos and the smell of death.

Ivar glanced right. The double doors into the nightclub stood wide open, one hanging off broken hinges. Ruined furniture—some intact, most missing legs and chair backs—littered the open area beyond the vestibule. Twin bars stood on either side of the room, facing off like foes, stools lying like dying soldiers in front of both, the identical antique mirrors backstopping each tarnished by time and now devastation. He strode past it all, coming to a stop at the edge of the dance floor. Moonlight bled onto the once glossy surface, shining through a gaping hole in the roof. Throat gone tight, Ivar hit his haunches, and shifting his weight, knelt amid the debris.

"I'm sorry. Please forgive me for failing you," he whispered, hearing the ache in his voice.

Raising the bottle of Jim Beam, he toasted his fallen comrades and drank deep. The whiskey burned on the way down and caught fire in his belly. Heat spread inside his chest. Ivar swallowed the pain, and filling his lungs to capacity, shouted each warrior's name. His voice rang out. His heart grew heavy, and yet he continued, honoring their memory in the way of his kind before tipping the mouth of the bottle toward the floor. Amber liquid poured out in a stream, splattering the hardwood as he drew a circle around himself. With a murmur, he let his magic roll. His dragon half responded, lighting the fuse, setting the ring of alcohol on fire in the center of the club.

Pink tendrils of flame dancing around him, Ivar pushed to his feet. "Rest well, my brothers. God grant you peace."

The reverent words echoed, reaching up to meet the night sky.

His duty done, Ivar tossed the bottle aside. Glass shattered. The sound cracked through the quiet as he tipped his head back. Gazing on the moon through the hole in the ceiling, he transformed, shifting from human to dragon form. Muscle and bone stretched beneath blood red scales. Hand and feet turning to talons, Ivar bared his fangs and snarled at the night sky. His growl rippled as he left the fire to burn, unfolded his wings, and leapt toward the soot smeared ceiling.

Blasting through what remained of Deuce's roof, he sent wood and steel flying like pick-up sticks. Wrapped in magic, hidden from human eyes by a cloaking spell, he climbed, rising above the cityscape, and turned north. Time to go home. Before grief got the better of him. Before his guilt became insurmountable. Before Denzeil—his pain in the ass second-in-command—noticed he wasn't in his laboratory and sent a squadron of Razorbacks—

Static exploded between his temples.

Ivar's sonar pinged. Rocketing around a skyscraper, he rotated into a tight spiral and waited for the deep voice to come through mind-speak. The equivalent of a cell phone for his kind, the cosmic connection worked like a charm, linking males who accepted one another over great distances. Magic expanded, then whiplashed, ghosting around the horns on his head. Any second now. A few more seconds and...ah, yes.

Here it came...interference with a capital I.

"*Boss-man,*" the voice said, echoing inside his skull.

Ah shit. So much for getting home before anyone noticed he was gone. "*What is it, D?*"

"*Where the hell are you?*"

"*In the lab.*"

"*Bullshit.*"

Inevitable. Denzeil might be a pain, but the male wasn't stupid. "*Really?*"

"*Ja,*" Denzeil said, reverting to his failsafe...German, his mother tongue. A habit of his whenever the warrior became annoyed. "*Particularly since I'm standing in your lab and you're not here.*"

He sighed. "*I'm on my way home.*"

A pregnant pause followed that statement, then...

"*Scheiße. You promised, Ivar. You promised you wouldn't—*"

"*Watch it, Denzeil,*" he said, soft tone full of warning. "*You are not my keeper.*"

"*I know, but you shouldn't be out on your own. The Nightfury pack—*"

"*Fuck the Nightfuries.*" An excellent sentiment. Now if only the enemy would die as planned. Not an easy thing to accomplish. Luckier than most, the Nightfuries were like cats. The assholes kept landing on their feet. "*Downtown is quiet. None of the bastards are around tonight.*"

"*Regardless...*" The sound of heavy footfalls came

through mind-speak. *"I'm coming out to meet you anyway."*

"Don't bother." Focused on the north end of the city, Ivar increased his wing speed. A blast of frigid air skimmed over him. The spikes along his spine rattled, providing a symphony of sound as tall buildings gave way to squat apartment buildings, leading him toward Suburbia. *"I'm a few minutes out."*

"Five minutes. I'm giving you five minutes, boss man, then I'm—"

"Yeah, yeah." Ivar growled, severing mind-speak.

The connection shattered. Static hissed, curling inside his ears as his warrior's voice faded along with the concern in his tone. Silence settled in like an old friend, rushing him across the night sky and over houses full of sleeping humans. Ivar exhaled in relief. Quiet was always welcome. Particularly when Denzeil went on the warpath, charging in on a worry rampage. Ivar huffed. Fucking male. Mother hen to the next power. Not that Ivar didn't appreciate the sentiment or that his warrior cared. He did. Well, most of the time anyway, but...

Jesus. Sometimes the babysitting routine got to be too much. And sometimes he needed to break away. To get out from beneath the yoke of leadership. To step away from the harsh reality of war and responsibility. To feel unencumbered, free of the weight he carried as commander of the Razorback Nation and just...live. Maybe even pretend all was right with his world.

At least, every once in a while.

Not too much to ask...right? Ivar nodded. His scales rattled, clicking together as he angled his wings, banking right to line up his final approach. His night vision sparked. Details sprang in pinpoint focus. A brick façade with wide windows and pale corner-stones flashed in the moon-glow up ahead. Ivar's mouth curved. Hmm, there it was...

28 Walton Street. Home sweet home.

Built in the 1950s, the old fire station anchored the entire neighborhood, rising about the tiny A-frame houses it sat alongside. Neglected for years, the property sat on thirteen glorious acres half an hour from downtown and still needed a helluva lot of work. Ivar didn't mind. He enjoyed challenges. Building the underground lair beneath the property had proven an excellent one. Almost complete, the subterranean lair he now called home was a thing of beauty—high-tech, sophisticated, and comfortable. But the absolute best part...the detail he loved most about his new digs? The complex operated on a closed electrical circuit. Was completely off the grid. No need to draw from city power sources. No reason to become involved with the human race. No carbon footprint to speak of, 100 percent eco-friendly and self-sustaining.

Just the way he liked it.

Flipping up and over, Ivar angled into the last turn. Icy air streaming from his wing-tips, he rocketed over an abandoned gas station. His eyes narrowed on the fire station two streets over. Almost there. One hundred and fifty feet out. X marked the spot on the blacktop in front of 28 Walton Street. Twin lines of reflective road paint flashed on asphalt below.

Ivar tucked his wings.

Gravity took hold, yanking him out of the sky. The chill of midnight blasted over his scales. He hummed, relishing the rush as his paws thumped down. An answering vibration rumbled along the street. Recycling bins sitting on the sidewalk jumped. Window glass rattled. Lamp posts swayed, making electrical cables click together. The cacophony of sound echoed, pinging off aluminum siding and cheap chain-link fences planted in front yards. Still cloaked in magic, Ivar froze in the middle of the street and listened hard, waiting for the racket to wake the neighborhood. Cold seeping into the pads of his paws, he glanced over his shoulder. Nada. Zero movement. No lights came on. No front doors opened. Not a peep from the sleepy section of Suburbia he called home.

Thank Jesus. The last think he needed was—

Beep-beep-honk! Whoop-whoop-screech!

Baring his fangs, Ivar whipped around as a car alarm went off. Spiked tail flying overhead, the tips of his claws gouged grooves in the asphalt, pushing jagged pebbles between his talons. He ignored the discomfort in favor of finding the source. His gaze narrowed on the banged up Jeep shrieking three houses down. Taillights flashed, lighting up the neighborhood. He clenched his teeth. Goddamn son of a whore. Not again. The mud-splattered POS doubling as a 4x4 went off every time he turned around. Tonight made...well, he didn't know how many times the stupid thing had gone off this week. Three? Four? Ivar frowned. He'd lost count after the old lady down the street called the cops and a black and white rolled up to give the owner a warning.

Ivar growled. Beyond annoying. The absolute worst kind of neighbor. Which meant the human who'd moved into the tidy little A-frame three weeks ago needed a lesson. A big one, and fast. Before the old lady complained again. Before the cops came back. Before human authorities looked too closely at the fire station and unearthed the underground complex beneath it. Swallowing a curse, Ivar shifted into human form, conjured his clothes, and stomping his feet into his shitkickers, started toward the rust bucket pretending to be a Jeep. No time like the present. He and his new neighbor were due for a chat.

Then again, maybe not.

Talking, after all, was overrated. Action suited him better. Violence too. Brutality got results like nothing else could, so...yeah. Maybe he'd go with plan B and snap the troublemaker's neck instead. Simple. Easy. Expedient. All components in a good strategy. Particularly since hiding the body—and getting rid of the vehicle—would prove no challenge at all.

2

Blind dates sucked. And on-line dating services? Slamming the front door behind her with a bang, Sasha Cooper sighed in disgust. Nothing but a cesspool full of bad intentions. Add a colossal waste of time to the mix and...yup. It was official.

Cupid hated her.

Tucking a strand of hair behind her ear, she tossed her purse onto the countertop in her kitchen, then just stood there in her sexy-as-sin, never-before-worn boots not knowing what to do. Shake her fist at the heavens? Tip her head back and scream in frustration? Take a magic marker to a picture of Cupid and draw horns on his head? The latter seemed like the best option. The effect of the devil, after all, suited the chubby beast better than a bow and arrow. The little prick. He refused to give her a break. Annoying as hell. Beyond exasperating. Unfair too. Sasha fingered her keys as she glanced toward the only handbag she owned—a knock-off, not at all her usual thing, but...

Jeez. She might as well admit it.

Date night changed a woman. Or maybe that was just her. Witness the fact she'd jumped on the short-skirt, stiletto-sporting, buy-a handbag-to-impress-a-man bandwagon this evening. Pathetic in more ways than one. Too bad there appeared to be no way around it. Not if she wanted to be the recipient of a man-made orgasm anytime soon.

With a sigh, Sasha shook her head and tossed her keys toward the fake Prada. Metal jingled in mid-air. The heavy key-ring thunked down and slid across the kitchen peninsula, coming to rest above a drawer that held a tray full of Sharpies. Her eyes narrowed on the tarnished drawer handle. One tug. A smooth reverse glide and...bam! Marker heaven. Every color of the rainbow within easy reach. Sasha pursed her lips. Never let it be said she wasn't prepared to deface the love god at moment's notice, cuz...yup. No doubt about it. Taking a marker to Cupid was looking better all the time considering she stood inside the tiny bungalow she rented instead of downtown Seattle getting her grove on with cyber-set-up number three.

Or rather, the man who might've turned out to be Mr. Right.

God, that sounded pitiful. Especially since the guy in question hadn't bothered to show up. No excuse sent by way of a text. No explanation delivered via email either. Grabbing her handbag by the neck, Sasha rifled through it, looking for her cell phone. Bright, shiny and new, the Samsung slid into her hand. As she pulled it free of faux leather, light from the nearby lamp bounced off its glossy face. Angling her hand to eliminate the glare, she tapped the touch screen. Nope. Still nothing. Not a single phone call, never mind a message saying "sorry, Sasha but I won't be able to make it tonight." Instead, she'd sat for nearly an hour inside an upscale restaurant, watching lovey-dovey couples while she fiddled with her wine glass, feeling foolish and alone, but mostly...

Unwanted.

A pang hit her chest level. All dressed up. Some place to go, but no one to be with. The story of her life lately.

Her brows furrowed, she stared harder at her phone, willing it to ring. Nothing happened. And no wonder. After midnight now, it was past the point of no return. Blind date number three—aka the jerk who'd stood her up—knew it too. Proof positive sat in her hand—not ringing. Which meant...wow...she'd sunk to an all time new low. Now guys she'd never even met were blowing her off. It shouldn't bother her. Really, it shouldn't, but even as she told herself one broken date didn't matter, her heart hitched and hurt rose. Resignation followed, making her wonder why she bothered. Sheer torture, plain and simple. And yet, she played the dating game anyway, putting herself in the line of fire, searching for meaningful connection...someone to love and be loved by in return.

Cinderella in the twenty-first century syndrome.

Sasha rubbed her temples, admitting she suffered from it. She'd bought into the fairytale years ago...the way five year old girls did when presented with a princess dress and the Disney channel. A pity, really. Futile in so many ways.

Particularly since the disease seemed to have metastasized in recent days. Fueled by a promise made to her best friend, the love bug was growing out of control, spreading into areas of her life that usually remained untouched.

Case in point? Her job versus the man distraction she carried to work every day.

"Stupid promise." Sasha glared at her phone. "I never should have agreed."

But she had, accepting the challenge over one too many margaritas, allowing her BFF to put her on-line profile up on e-whatever-it-was-called. More fool her. Not anywhere near her usual MO either. She never caved beneath the pressure applied by her soon-to-be-married best friend. Sasha scowled. Damn Lily and her harebrained idea anyway. Her friend was wrong. She didn't need a man. All right, so maybe she wanted one—secretly, covertly, with a longing buried deep in the recesses of her Disney-obsessed brain—but *need* wasn't part of the equation. Smart. Strong. Independent. She ticked all the boxes, putting the word *go* into go-getter. Which...come to think of it...might be part of the problem on the find-a-man-front.

Not that her boss complained about her abysmal social life.

Dr. Preston appreciated her ambition and drive. Her passion for the environment too. Wildlife ecology —and the conservation projects she spearheaded and supervised—required all three. So did the Washington Department of Fish and Wildlife. Half-assed wasn't in the job description. Neither was part-time. Sasha huffed in wary amusement. Make that full-time plus, plus...*plus*. An eighty hour work week was the rule, not the exception. To be expected. At least, for her. As lead scientist attached to the research division, she spent weeks in the field, setting up surveillance, collecting data on fauna and environmental erosion all over the state.

Not that she minded the long absences.

Or the time and energy she expended hiking in and out of remote locations to check on her equipment. A perk of the job. Science required dedication, and saving endangered species from ecological devastation, true focus. Which left little time for anything else. Like oh say, landing a man and getting laid. The dreaded dry spell spoke volumes. Eighteen months and counting. Not that she was counting, but...ah frig. Who was she kidding? *She* was counting. So was Lily, which naturally prompted the month long dating challenge.

God. St. Valentine's Day couldn't come soon enough.

February 14th. All she needed to do was make it to V-day, then she'd be free. Emancipated from the evil clutches of e-what's-its-name. Able to wipe her face—along with her profile—off the internet forever and return to the life she knew and loved. Except...

Someone just shoot her, 'cause...curse it all. That was a bald-faced lie. No one liked being alone. And despite her vehement denials to the contrary, neither did she.

Grumbling under her breath, Sasha scrolled through the list of contacts on her phone. Finding the right one, she tapped the screen. The Samsung paused, then went to work, ringing in her ear. With a smooth shoulder roll, she shrugged out of her leather jacket. Cool air caressed her exposed skin. Goose bumps rose beneath her slinky wrap dress. Ignoring the chill, she skirted the kitchen peninsula, tossed her coat over a breakfast bar stool, and high heels clicking on hardwood, walked into her living room. Instant relief. Open plan layout and ready comfort punctuated by a slip-covered couch, a cozy armchair, and teak end tables. White on white with warm wood accents. Shabby chic perfection. Easy living in a small space that boasted loads of charm.

Sasha's mouth curved. Wham, bam, thank you

ma'am real estate broker.

The bungalow might be a small one bedroom, but it ran the line right into perfection. Such a surprise. The ultimate find in a tight rental market and the best of all worlds—renovated by the owner, close to Sasha's office, a real 1950s gem. And love at first sight when she'd visited a month ago. Lily still thought she'd lost her mind. Sasha begged to differ. Living downtown had been fun for a while, but big city life wasn't for her. She preferred quaint and quiet. So when her lease on the condo ended—and Lily moved out to live with her fiancé—Sasha made the leap, getting the hell out of Dodge and the downtown core.

The phone clicked in her ear. A familiar voice came over the line. "Please tell me you're about to get laid."

"Depends," Sasha said, flopping down in the middle of the couch. Deep-seated cushions hugged her from behind. She slid into a slouch, enjoying the abundance of thick-fluffy-and comfortable, and stared up at the tongue-and-groove ceiling. "Does my pulsating showerhead count?"

"Ah crap. You're home alone."

"Uh-huh."

"What happened?"

Sasha shrugged even though her friend couldn't see her. "He didn't show."

"Damn."

"Yeah." Crossing one leg over the other, Sasha studied the toe of her fancy boot. Not that the pair was expensive. Like her handbag, the knee-highs were knock-offs. Pretty convincing ones done up in black leather with suede accents and three inch heels, but...nah. The matching set had nothing on real Guccis. Fine by her. She preferred her hiking boots anyway. Much more comfortable, not to mention practical. Particularly since it looked as though a man-made orgasm wasn't on the menu...or anywhere near her immediate future. "Blind dates...sooo unreliable. Who knew, right?"

Lily sighed, the harsh exhale unhappy. "Men are idiots."

A masculine voice grumbled, coming through the speaker.

"Not you, babe," Lily said, reassuring the boy toy she called fiancé. And Sasha called Ben. A good guy, great catch, and all around perfect boyfriend to her BFF. The two were joined at the hip, so content it made Sasha's heart pang and envy make an unscheduled stop inside her head. Not that she wasn't thrilled for Lily. She was...without question. Her friend deserved the best of the best, but even as happiness for Lily rose, Sasha couldn't deny the truth. She wanted a happily-ever-after of her own. "I meant single guys, Ben. You're perfect, of course."

"Pukesville, Lil."

"Eat your heart out, Sash," her friend said, a grin in her voice. "You're just cranky 'cause you're not getting any."

True enough. "That's me...totally orgasm deprived."

Lily laughed. Ben mumbled something in the background. "You know, babe...that's not a bad idea."

Uh-oh. Not good. The wonder couple was ganging up on her. "Don't tell me what he just said. I really don't want to know."

Her smart-ass best friend ignored her. "Ben thinks you should just go out and get laid."

Sasha blinked. "What?"

"You know...have a one night stand."

"You want me to sleep with a stranger?"

Ben got up close and personal with the phone. "It would solve the orgasm deprivation problem."

Sasha snorted.

"Hang on, Sash. Not so fast," Lily said, enthusiasm in her tone, warming to her fiancé's idiotic idea. "Forget the dating scene for a minute. New mission strategy."

Oh God. Someone please shoot her...right now. "I don't think—"

"Perfect." Something creaked as Ben moved. A second later, a rustle that sounded suspiciously like cotton sheets came over the airwaves. Sasha sighed. Terrific. Just wonderful. The pair were in bed...no doubt about to do the nasty. Again. She should be accustomed to it by now. Every time Sasha called her friend at home she caught them in one of three positions—in the middle of the act, about to do the act, or breathing hard from just having completed the act. God help her. "Don't think. Go get your rocks off instead."

"You're a lunatic, Ben."

"Yeah, but a sexually satisfied one," he said, laughing at her. "You on the other hand—"

"Oh, shut up."

With a chuckle, Lily stole the phone back. "Why not, Sasha?"

The question unearthed her imagination. Sex with a stranger. Sasha bit down on her bottom lip. Was her best friend serious? Probably. The queen of one night stands in college, Lily didn't suffer from compunction. At least, not of the sexual variety. Her friend always followed her fancy, did as she pleased along with anyone she wanted. Raised to be a good girl instead of a free spirit, Sasha had never been sexually adventurous. In her mind, sex equaled commitment. But that wasn't true, was it? Women slept with men and walked away all the time. Easy-peasy...no strings attached. No guilt or the least bit of shame involved.

An interesting concept. Completely taboo. A fantasy in the making.

All right, so it sat on the far edge of her comfort zone, but well...

Sasha pushed away from the couch back. Sex with a smokin' hot stranger. Sex without any strings. Sex, sex, nothing but sex, so help her God...free and clear in the morning. Perched on the edge of the seat cushion, knees pressed together, she frowned. Holy crap. She was actually thinking about it—wondering, imagining...fantasizing about the guy she would pick out of a crowd. Weird, but...she could picture it. See the scene unfolding in her mind's eye. Frame by frame. Each touch. Every sigh. All the pleasure as she—

"Look, it's the twenty-first century, sweetie. You're allowed to have a little fun," Lily said, tempting her. Urging Sasha to be as adventurous in her love life as she was in her job. "Drop the good girl complex and be a bad girl for a change. Grab the first guy you're attracted to, go dancing all night, then take him home. Be smart about it, but..."

Ben's deep voice rumbled again.

Sasha cringed, bracing for another explicit suggestion and...gosh darn it all... more temptation. 'Cause yeah. With the seed planted, Sasha admitted its allure, and that the idea was also starting to grow—expand, take on a life of its own inside her head.

"Oh, right...thanks babe. Good suggestion." Lily paused to give her fiancé a smacking kiss. Static hissed as she put the phone back to her ear. "Ben says to make sure he's not married first."

Excellent advice. The best, really. Particularly if she decided to go through with—

Beep-beep-honk! Whoop-whoop-screech!

Popping to her feet, Sasha tittered on her high heels. "Crap."

"What is it?" Lily asked.

"Gotta go. My Jeep's going ballistic again." Gaze locked on the keychain half hidden behind her purse on the countertop, Sasha hightailed it around the armchair. "Call you later."

With a quick touch to the screen, she hung up on her best friend. No time to talk, never mind finish the sex-with-a-stranger conversation. She needed to grab her keys and get out the front door. Right now. Before her car alarm woke up the entire neighborhood. Otherwise, crotchety Mrs. Crowley would call the cops on her again and...

Oh man. Not a good idea. Neither was dallying.

Her new neighbor might be eighty-two years young, but she was fast on her feet. And even quicker on the trigger. The old fox was no doubt already out of bed, stick-thin form bundled in a bathrobe, fuzzy pink slippers doing double time as she ran for her rotary phone. In a flap, Sasha raced past the trio of stools and skidded around the end of the peninsula. Tossing her phone onto the counter, she grabbed her keys on the fly-by, and without missing a beat, headed for the door.

Bright light from the Jeep's headlights lit up the kitchen window.

Flash on. Blink off. *Beep-beep-honk! Whoop-whoop-screech!*

"Shit, shit...shit!"

Stupid car alarm. Persnickety to the point of demonic possession, the thing went off all the time. But

worse? The aftermarket system refused to deactivate
unless she stood within ten feet of it. She pressed the
red button anyway, thumb working overtime. Nothing
yet, but as soon as she stepped outside, it would quit.

She hoped.

One never knew when dealing with the eight-year-
old vehicle she drove into rough terrain on a regular
basis. Banged up and rusted in spots, her Wrangler
had seen better days. Sasha didn't care. She loved her
4x4, dents, scratches and all. Only one problem—the
cheap car alarm her mechanic had installed. She really needed to do something about that...like kill the
idiotic thing, just yank it right out by its electronic go-
nads and be done with the drama. Heart hammering
the inside of her chest, Sasha slid to a stop in front of
the door. Still pressing the button as if her life de-
pended on it, she palmed the handle, yanked the door
open and—

Ran straight into a man.

"Holy crap!" Jumping in surprise, Sasha
backpedaled.

Hand raised to knock on her door, her visitor
rocked back on his heels. "Fucking hell."

Well, that was one way of putting it.

Another would be wow. Add YUM to the package
and...uh-huh. She had a winner, 'cause holy Hannah
on a swizzle stick, he was flat out gorgeous. Big, bad
and sculpted, at least six and a half feet of male glory.
Sexy as hell too, with black sun-glasses shielding his
eyes. The wraparounds did wonders for his face, en-
hancing his angular features, accenting his dark red
hair, giving him an edge that screamed "I'm great in
bed."

Her libido purred in appreciation.

Instant attraction lit the fuse. Curiosity collided

with arousal. Sasha looked him over again. Faded jeans encasing long legs. Scuffed boots on his feet. White T-shirt stretched over a muscular chest and wide shoulders, beaten up leather jacket over the whole. Forcing her lungs to unlock, she took a deep breath and...sweet Mary. He smelled fantastic too, like exotic spice, dark fantasies and...mercy. Mr. Tall-Dark-and-Dangerous. He looked the part, and her imagination took flight. Naughty thoughts filtered in. Ones that circled around sex and the fact he was most certainly a stranger.

The car alarm shrieked again.

Still staring at him, Sasha extended her arm over the threshold and pressed the button. Headlights stopped flashing.

Silence descended, cranking her tight, making her wonder and imagine and...ache from the inside out. Taut muscles pulled at her abdomen. Sensation spiraled out, sending shivers up her spine and tingles to interesting places. She swallowed past a bad case of dry mouth. Gaze pinned to hers, he dropped his hand and leaned toward her. Not a lot. The movement was slight, more subtle shift than true displacement. But Sasha knew what it meant. Along with what he wanted. Call it woman's intuition, but...

He was as interested in her as she was in him.

Her gaze dropped to his lips. Great mouth. Full, masculine...made for kissing. Her heart picked up a beat, and then another. Sasha listened to the blood rush and blew out a pent-up breath. Should she...or shouldn't she? An excellent question. One she'd never asked before when it came to sex. But as the silence expanded and the cold drifted in through the open door, Sasha wanted to be brave. Just this once. Maybe Lily was right. Maybe she needed to let loose and live a little. Maybe the man standing on her doorstep was what she needed. A sexual adventure wrapped up in sinew and bone, so...

To hell with it. Time to take a risk along with a leap of faith.

"Are you married?"

Dark brows collided behind his Oakleys. "Nyet."

The Russian word rolled on his deep voice. Oh God. Hot as hell and a sexy accent. Cupid must love her, after all.

She'd just hit the jackpot. "Good."

He opened his mouth—no doubt to ask if she'd lost her mind.

Sasha didn't give him a chance. With a quick step forward, she fisted her hands in his leather jacket and tugged. The move caught him off guard. She yanked again, and knuckles pressed to the wall of his chest, pulled him off balance. He stumbled over the threshold. She slammed the door in his wake. A growl—the sound low and lethal, yet somehow full of welcome—rumbled up his throat. Bolstered by his reaction, Sasha popped onto her tiptoes, and fingers sifting through his hair, licked his bottom lip. He tensed in surprise. Sasha refused to back down. She needed a taste. Of pleasure. Of passion. Of the desire she'd kept under wraps for far too long. After that, he could do as he pleased. Push her away. Pull her close. Make love to her until she fell into pleasure-bound oblivion.

Totally up to him.

Either way, she was desperate to feel. Something. Anything. His hard body against hers—his kiss...hot, wet and deep—would do the trick. So yeah, like it or not, one way or the other, Mr. Tall-Dark-and-Dangerous was going to give her everything she asked for. And exactly what she wanted.

3

O ff balance, Ivar stumbled over the threshold and into the female's arms. Senses honed by years of war, he fell into habit and scanned the layout over the top of her head. Small kitchen. Open plan set up. No threat in sight.

Thank fuck. He didn't know what he would've done had the enemy been standing in the middle of her living room.

Died, most likely 'cause...man. He couldn't think straight. Not with her all over him. Sweet feminine curves—all the soft skin pressed up against him—negated brain function, shoving him in one direction. Toward blind lust. Into raging need. Distracting him with a hunger so intense he wanted to fall in with the plan. Consequences be damned.

Not smart. Or anywhere near advisable.

Ivar knew it. Kept telling himself being this close to another without any intel was a bad idea, but...hmm. She was incredible. So soft in his arms. So beautiful with her blonde hair messed up and desire shining in her dark brown eyes.

Her mouth brushed the corner of his. He swallowed a sudden case of dry mouth and tried to hang on. To do the right thing—the smart thing—and back away. More information. He needed some right now. Before it all went to hell and she—

Popping up on her tiptoes, the female nipped his bottom lip.

Bliss whispered his name. His body went haywire, short circuiting, hardening so fast his mind went blank. Reflex made his hands tighten on her waist. "Shit. Hold on a second, just—"

"Kiss me back."

Oh, Jesus. That voice. The husky timbre of *her voice* hit all the right notes, playing across his senses, stroking over nerve endings already frayed by her touch. Pleasure sank deep. Male appreciation spiked, spiraling into desire, killing more brain cells. She murmured, and inviting him to kiss her, buried her hands in his hair. Ecstasy followed in the wake of her caress, urging him to forget his training and step into the fray. Into her and accept what she offered. It would be so easy to do. Effortless, really. Beyond good to simply let go and be a male instead of the commander of warriors. At least, for a little while.

Temptation urged him forward. Instinct held him back.

Something was off. Way, way out in left field. Females didn't invite him—or rather...drag him—into their homes. Not for sex or anything else. Most kept their distance, giving him a wide berth, only coming near when he encouraged them into his sphere. This one, though, hadn't gotten the memo. She wasn't afraid of him...at all. Her body language and scent said it all. She wanted him. Was already aroused and ready to take him every step of the way. Unprecedented. Surprising too, considering the lethal vibe he carried around like luggage. Not that she noticed. Or maybe that wasn't it. Maybe she simply didn't care. Some women enjoyed danger, the thrill of the hunt along with the idea of getting down and dirty with a bad boy.

A good theory. One he could work with as she pressed her advantage, used his confusion against him, and kissed him again. With a hum, she licked into his mouth. Her taste hit him like a body shot. Ivar groaned and lost ground. Unable to say no—or push her away—he got in on the action and touched his tongue to hers. She purred, the sound full of satisfaction, and shoved him backward. His shoulder blades bumped the door at his back. Clever fingers stroking over his nape, she played with his hair, getting as close as clothes allowed. Which was...

Fascinating. Enthralling. Beyond good or anything he'd felt while holding a female.

The thought sent him sideways inside his own head, adding to his confusion. Something about her was...shit. He didn't know exactly. But instinct warned him she was special. A gift in many ways. Someone to be wary of in others. Particularly since the Meridian— the electrostatic bands that ringed the planet, the source of all living things—reacted, opening a channel deep inside him. Energy bled through the fissure, making his temples buzz and his fingertips tingle. Ivar frowned as the current amplified. Testing the sensation, he deepened the kiss.

Awareness exploded, spilling into delight.

She moaned. His heart picked up a beat. And then another, slamming the inside of his chest as he became addicted to the soft sounds she made. The instant the bliss-filled hum ended, he wanted to hear it again. And again. All of a sudden, close wasn't close enough. He longed to be skin-to-skin with her.

Wanted her to moan his name as he took himself to new heights in her arms. Such a dangerous thought. His reaction to her—and the impulse that drove it— wasn't safe. Not at all the norm when he touched a female.

And far too messy.

He craved order. Liked things neat. Preferred tidy, and by extension, mistrusted anything he couldn't control. Danger lived in the outliers—in the wilds of human compulsion where impulse control became a problem. Clearly an issue for him at the moment. But God, she was a prime piece. So hot. So needy. So beautiful as she demanded without words that he please her. Temptation grabbed hold. Experience settled him down. He refused to lose himself in her heat.

Not yet anyway.

Walking into the unknown never ended well. He needed to understand first. Wanted to know why. The reason he'd gone from standing outside the door— from pissed off and prepared to scare the hell out of his neighbor—to, well *this*...deep seated desire driven by the female now kissing him blind. Which meant...

Time to take control of the situation. And her.

Planting his feet on the entryway rug, Ivar righted his balance and lifted his head. She protested with a murmur. Her grip on him tightened, the message clear...*kiss me again*. Another round of need roared through him. Ivar shook his head, and staring down at her from behind his wraparounds, leaned away. Eyes half hidden behind her lashes, she tugged harder. Baring his teeth, he reversed their positions, making her gasp as he shoved his thigh between her own, and pressed her back to the door.

Her lips parted on an adorable little "O". Shoulder blades flat against the wood panel, controlled now by him, she tipped her chin up. One hand still buried in his hair, the other slid around to stroke along his jaw. "You taste good. Come back."

"Tell me your name first."

Mischief sparked in her eyes. She shook head. "No names. Let's keep it anonymous, okay?"

Ivar's eyes narrowed behind his Oakleys. No, not okay. Nothing about his encounter with her would be *anonymous*. Whether she knew it or not, he would know everything about her before he finished. So yeah. He wanted her name before he went any further. First. Last. Every hope and dream attached to her too...along with the reason she'd dragged him inside her home.

Holding her immobile, he took off his sunglasses. Her breath caught. He held steady, refusing to look away even though he knew what she was seeing. Pink irises, unusual enough in the Dragonkind gene pool, almost non-existent in the human world. Well, except in lab rats and albinos.

Of which, he was neither.

"Your eyes," she whispered, her gaze steady on his. Needing to see her reaction, Ivar let her look. Most ran scared when they saw his eyes. The blonde, however, surprised him. Instead of trying to get away, she lifted her hand, and touch gentle, traced the curve of his eyebrow with her fingertip. "But you're not an albino."

Smart as well as beautiful. A stirring combination, one that made him want her more. "How do you know?"

"Steady pigment. Normal skin color," she said, awe in her voice, something close to scientific interest in her eyes.

Changing course, she caressed the day old stubble

on his jaw. Red whiskers, the same color as the hair on his head. "You're a genetic anomaly."

In her world, maybe. He was 100 percent normal in his. "Do you care?"

"No."

"Then tell me why I'm here."

"Guess."

"Lay it out for me instead." A touch cruel, perhaps, but he wanted to hear her say it. Needed her to admit her need and ask him to assuage it. But as she squirmed, struggling to find the right words, silence stretched between them. She opened, then closed her mouth...twice. Amused by her speechlessness, Ivar took pity and raised a brow. "You looking for a fast fuck with a complete stranger?"

The crude language made her flinch.

Shock flared in her eyes a second before her face heated. Crimson spread in a glorious wave across her cheekbones. Ivar went still as he watched her. Instinct spiked. All kinds of assumptions followed. His mouth curved. Well, would you look at that? Little Ms. Aggressive was just a teensy bit shy. Which told him more than he needed to know. Good girl gone bad. She carried all the markers. He could smell it on her, the need to go rogue, if only for one night.

"Tell me true, kitten." Shifting against her, he glanced over his shoulder. With a flick, he tossed his Oakleys across the kitchen. The pair landed on the countertop, then slid, colliding with her purse as he returned his attention to her. Wide brown eyes met his. "Is that what you want from me? Are you going to open up and let me all the way in...deep, deep inside?"

Her blush deepened, but she didn't back down. She nodded instead.

"No anonymity, then. Give me your name."

"Sasha."

"Pretty name," he murmured, giving into a smile. He couldn't help it. She was perfect. So beautiful with her pale skin and dark eyes. And her name. God, it was perfect too. Of Russian origin, a name he could say with relish. One that reminded him of home and happier times, of things long forgotten until now. Cupping her cheek, he caressed her bottom lip with the pad of his thumb, then leaned in and kissed her. A gentle touch. Hardly a kiss at all. The mere brush of his mouth against hers. "Ivar."

"Nice to meet you, Ivar." Tone naughty, his name rolled off her tongue. Pleasure skittered down his spine. Lips curved up at the corners, she shifted on his thigh, and undulating against him, showed him what she wanted. "Now, if you don't mind..."

Ivar didn't. Not even a little. He was all in. Willing to play the game, completely committed to her pleasure as long as he received some in return. "Fast or slow the first time, Sasha?"

She blinked in surprise. "The first time?"

"You invited me in, kitten," he said, giving her fair warning. "I'm not leaving until I get my fill, so...fast or slow?"

A fine tremor rolled through her. "Fast."

"As you wish."

He murmured the words against her mouth. His tone said acquiesce. His touch, however, said something else. Dominant to the core, Ivar took over. Kissing her deep, he fisted his hands in her skirt. A quick tug pulled it up her torso. A firmer yank drew the soft material over her head and...Jesus help him. She'd dressed to kill tonight. Silky dress. Sexy high-heeled boots. But the most incredible sight lay underneath—silk and lace holding creamy skin and abundant curves. So soft. So warm and sweet. A gift wrapped up in black satin topped with pretty pink bows.

Throat gone tight, Ivar fingered the one perched between her breasts, then traced the lace over the top of her gorgeous curve. Caressing her with a gentle stroke, he dipped inside the demi-cup, gauging her sensitivity, fighting to stay in control as her nipple tightened beneath the satin. Her breath caught on his name. Hearing it sent him into a tailspin. God forgive him, but she was right. The first time was going to be fast. Crazy and wild...far too fucking fast.

But he couldn't help it.

He wanted her too much to back off. Or slow down. He couldn't control it, so he sank into sensation instead. The work of moments, he stripped her bare— tossing the dress over his shoulder, unclasping her bra, releasing her long enough to drag the frilly panties down her thighs. The second he freed her, he pressed her back to the wall. Moaning in welcome, Sasha wrapped her legs around his hips, and setting her mouth to his, slid her hands down his chest. She shoved at his jacket. Eager to please, Ivar shrugged it off his shoulders. Heavy leather hit the floor as she attacked his T-shirt. Raising his arms, he helped her tug it over his head. Her hands touched down, stroking over his skin, fracturing what little remained of his control. A quick adjustment. An easy shift, and he yanked the button-fly of his jeans open, cupped her bottom and—

"Ivar!"

Sasha gasped as he thrust deep. Bliss stuck like a mailed fist. Ivar groaned. Oh Jesus. Fucking hell. Sasha was more than perfect. She was unbelievable. So incredible she cracked him wide open, tearing at his restraint as he sank between her thighs, and she struggled to accept him. All of him...every last inch he fed her. Clenching his teeth, he forced himself to slow down. She was so tight. Much smaller than he'd expected and...God. He didn't want to hurt her. Or rush her into acceptance. Which left him with only one option...wait for her to adjust to his invasion. A strange reaction. Especially coming from him. Caring wasn't part of his MO. He took what he wanted...always hit hard and moved fast.

Show no mercy. Give no quarter. His approach in a nutshell.

But as Sasha trembled in his arms, something odd happened. He didn't want the sex to be that way this time. Not with her. Instead of fast and hard, he wanted to treat her well. To be kind and patient for a change. To give her all the pleasure she deserved, and he wasn't accustomed to providing. A novelty wrapped up in a new experience. One Ivar couldn't deny. So instead of taking care of himself, he held still, ignoring the urge to move. Brushing the blonde tendrils away from her temple, he cradled her close and set his mouth to the corner of hers.

"Sasha."

Eyes squeezed shut, she quivered against him.

"Easy," he murmured, kissing her gently, coaxing her into acceptance. He needed her to move first. The second she relaxed—shifted the slightest bit—he'd know she was ready for him and the ride...for every ounce of ecstasy he wanted to give her. "Look at me, kitten."

"Give me a minute. I'm just...and you're really..."

"Big?"

"Egomaniac," she whispered, a smile in her voice. "Typical man."

"Satisfaction guaranteed," he said, teasing her while he tested her tension.

Almost there. It wouldn't be long now. Thread by taut thread, Sasha let go, relaxing against him, making his heart swell and his pride for her grow as she put herself in his care.

"I hope so," she said with a wiggle, adjusting their fit. "Otherwise, I wouldn't have dragged you inside."

Ivar huffed in amusement. Tightening her grip on him, Sasha squirmed again. He clenched his teeth and bore down, killing the urge to move. Not yet. Jesus...*not yet*. She needed more time, but as she opened her eyes, giving him what he wanted—loads of eye contact —Ivar almost lost it. Sasha didn't help him gain control. Breathing hard, looking sexy as hell, she tipped her chin, demanding another kiss. He shook his head, refusing to give her one. He couldn't and hope to stay in control. The second her mouth touched his, it would be over and...

He would be moving, thrusting hard and fast to her center.

Caressing the tops of his shoulders, she sent prickles of pleasure through him. "So you gonna show me now?"

"Are you ready to let me?"

Fisting her hands in his hair, she rocked against him. "God yes. So ready."

"Then ask me nicely." One hand beneath her bottom, Ivar drew the other along the outside of her thigh. Using the wall for leverage, he cupped the back of her knee, pushed it up and out, opening her wider. Her breath hitched as he slid all the way home, burying himself to the hilt inside her. "Beg me for the pleasure."

Caught between him and the wall, she twitched. "You have got to be kidding me."

"Dead serious."

"I don't beg."

"You will with me." Swirling his hips, he gave her a taste, teasing her with the promise of pleasure. She moaned, the sound so full of need Ivar almost gave in. *Almost*...but not quite. Call him a bastard, but he wanted her to surrender. All the way. No holds barred. Desire unleashed—her craving him as much as he did her, so...fuck it. He would hold her on the razor's edge. Refuse to provide what she demanded until he got what he needed first. "Give me my due, Sasha, and I'll give you yours."

Silence expanded a second before her lips parted. Her sharp inhale signaled shock. The excitement in her eyes indicated something else—deep seated arousal. The kind no female could resist. Ivar's mouth curved. Good girl, his ass. Sasha might like to pretend, but she enjoyed a good tussle. Was getting off on his dominant nature and the thought of what he might make her do. Which meant...

Time to add more fuel to her fire.

His gaze locked on hers, Ivar grasped her elbows. With a quick shift, he pumped his hips and shackled her wrists in one hand. As she gasped, arching into the half-thrust, he pinned her arms to the wall above her head, and leaned away.

His chest left her breasts. Cool air rushed in, raising goose bumps on her skin. He flexed his spine, pressing between the spread of her thighs. She keened, begging him without words to take her. But he needed the words, so instead of setting a steady rhythm, he dipped his head and—

"Oh my God!"

Bathing her in heat, Ivar licked her nipple again. Spine bowed in supplication, unable to move, she moaned. Showing no mercy, he settled in, suckling the gorgeous bud, fanning her flames, prepping her to beg. Panting now, she pulsed deep inside, tightening around him and...oh yeah. She was close. So fucking close. Almost ready to forsake her pride, so needy she wouldn't be able to hold out much longer. Circling the tight tip with his tongue, he switched sides to lavish its mate with equal attention.

Muscles quivering, Sasha squirmed in desperation.

"Submit, kitten." Ivar sucked harder, drawing out the pleasure. "Ask me nicely."

He nipped her gently. Her breath caught. "Please."

"Say my name."

"Please, Ivar."

The throaty plea unleashed him. The principles holding him in check snapped.

With a snarl, he released her hands, raised his head, and invaded her mouth. She met him halfway, tangling their tongues, tasting him deep as he withdrew and came back. He set a fast pace, riding her hard, gauging her pleasure, feeding her bliss one mind-blowing thrust at a time. And Sasha...God, she didn't disappoint. Passion incarnate, she met him stroke for stoke. Long legs wrapped around his waist, she sent her clever hands roaming, heightening his delight with her touch, egging him on with the sounds she made, deepening his possession with each flex and release of her hips.

Glorious friction. Incredible heat. Beautiful oblivion.

Unlike any he'd ever experienced.

Heart pounding, Ivar groaned as the pressure

mounted. Sasha cried out, begging him to push her over the edge. He upped the pace, driving her toward climax. Time stretched, one second spilling into the next. Ecstasy whiplashed, and she exploded, throbbing hard around him. Gritting his teeth, Ivar tried to hold on—to prolong the pleasure and her bliss—but she came again. And then again, squeezing him so tight he lost control. With a roar, Ivar detonated, cresting on a wave of delight so devastating he forgot everything. Past, present and future ceased to exist. In that moment, nothing mattered but her. Her scent on his skin. Him deep inside her. The beat of her heart and the awe in her voice as she gasped his name, and he sank to the floor with her in his arms.

4

Naked and tangled up with a man, Sasha lay on the floor in her kitchen, trying to catch her breath. Opening her eyes would be good too, but...God. One thing at a time. A girl could only manage so much. Recovery after the great sex—and three explosive orgasms—after all, took more than just a few minutes. Almost seven, as it turned out. Cracking her eyes open, she hugged Ivar closer, and raising her head off the braided rug, glanced toward the oven display. A blurry collection of numbers wavered in her line of sight. She blinked, hoping to clear her vision and...

The digital clock sprang into focus.

Uh-huh. She had lift off along with an accurate post-sex count. Forget seven. They'd just rounded the corner and hit the nine minute mark. Kind of nice, actually. She liked the feel of his arms around her. Was enjoying the cuddle along with the fact she lay half beneath him, one leg slung over his jean-clad hip, her hand still buried in his hair, his face pressed against the side of her throat. Sasha sighed and let her head fall back onto the rug. Lord, he was beautiful. So strong in all the right places. Great in bed too. A serious bonus considering her orgasm deprived status. Oh, wait.

Make that past tense, 'cause...wow. In one round, he'd given her a crazy amount of pleasure. Almost more than she'd been able to handle.

Not that she was complaining.

She'd needed a shove to get past her shyness. And a man who knew what he was doing. Ivar had provided both the push and the pleasure, wielding his expertise without mercy, making her meet him head-on, encouraging her to let go and bare all. Which explained why she was naked and Ivar still wore his pants...and boots. The realization tickled her funny bone. Her mouth curved against the top of his shoulder. God, she was shameless, a real—

"What's so funny?" he asked, nuzzling her pulse point.

Sasha shivered in delight. "Just reflecting."

He raised his head. Brushing the damp hair away from her temple, he met her gaze. "On?"

"How good you are at this."

"Sex?" When she nodded, satisfaction flashed in his eyes, making pink irises touched by gold shimmer a little. A trick of the light, no doubt, bu...Sasha bit her bottom lip. The glimmer was still odd, more than a touch left of center.

Lowering his lashes, he stared at her lips, hesitated a moment as though uncertain, then dipped his head. His mouth brushed hers. She opened, inviting him in, returning his kiss with a hum. "Hmm, well..." Nipping her gently, he pressed his thigh between her own and retreated just enough to look at her. "I've had lots of practice."

"Thank God for that."

He laughed, straight teeth flashing in the low light.

His delight triggered hers. Feeling lighter of spirit than she had in ages, she grinned at him. "Are you hungry?"

"For you...yes."

She huffed, so pleased with him she could hardly contain it. "I meant for food."

"Got any ice cream?"

"I'm a woman, Ivar," she said, tracing the ridge of his cheekbone with her fingertips. "I always have ice cream."

Amusement in his eyes, he shook his head. Palming his shoulder, Sasha gave him a playful shove. He complied, rolling off her and onto his back. She shifted in a hurry, and pressing her hand to his chest, popped to her feet. She landed without making a sound, one foot planted on either side of his hips, and stood over him. The position smacked of dominance. Something Sasha knew she would never be but...hmm. It was nice to pretend, if only for a moment. Especially with Ivar staring at her. His expression said it all. He found her beautiful. Liked too that she stood her ground, refusing to let shyness win, allowing him to look his fill. And he did, leaving none of her untouched as his gaze roamed over her breasts and belly, tracking south over private curls.

Her breath caught as his mouth parted. Anticipation tightened its grip, rumbling through her as she read his intent. The heat in his eyes gave it away. Now she knew what he was thinking. Next time he made love to her it wouldn't happen fast. Which meant, he'd have plenty of time to do what his gaze promised and...

Taste the curls between her thighs.

"Ice cream first," he murmured, giving her the distinct impression he'd just read her mind.

The thought circled inside her head, but lost speed when Ivar planted a hand on the floor and pushed to his feet. Taut muscles flexed in an impressive show of strength. Sasha bit the inside of her lip and stepped back, giving him room to maneuver in the small space, but didn't look away. Mercy, he was something. A rare sight with his bare chest on display and button-fly wide open, jeans hanging low on his lean hips.

"God, you're gorgeous," she whispered, mouth running away with her brain.

"All the better to please you with, my dear."

Sasha rolled her eyes and turned toward the fridge. "Turning into the big bad wolf, are you?"

"Maybe," he murmured from right behind her. So close. Barely an inch away. Within striking distance while he played the big bad wolf to perfection, crowding her without touching. Warm and minty sweet, his breath ghosted across the nape of her neck. Frissons of awareness exploded down her spine, making Sasha conscious of how much bigger he was than her. And that he could hurt her...if she let him. "Would you like that, Sasha?"

"I don't like it rough," she said, reaching for the freezer handle. A hard tug, and the door opened with a suctioning hiss. Nerve endings on fire, throat gone tight, Sasha grabbed a pint of strawberry ice cream, then glanced over her shoulder. Her gaze collided with his. She warned him with a look. "Don't go there, Ivar."

Mischief and something more—respect maybe?—flared in his eyes. "Fair enough, kitten."

She pointed to the cabinets behind him. "Spoons...third drawer from the right."

With a nod, he turned toward the peninsula and

went hunting. Silverware rattled in the utensil tray. The drawer closed with a bang. With a quick pivot, Ivar spun back toward her, and grabbing hold, picked her up. Sasha yelped as her feet left the floor. She bobbled the ice cream, playing hot potato with the cold container as he swung her into his arms. Cradled against him, she opened her mouth to protest. Ivar shook his head and put himself in gear. Five strides took them into the living room. Skirting the armchair, he sidestepped the coffee table, and doing an about face, sat in the middle of the couch. Plump cushions sighed, accepting his weight as he settled her astride him—bottom against his thighs, knees hugging his hips, core pressed to his button-fly.

Surprise stepped aside, making room for arousal. Sasha blinked. "Wow."

"Quick when I want to be, Sasha."

No kidding. Downright sneaky too...in a hot caveman kind of way.

The devil in his eyes, he held hers for a moment, then reached out, and took the *Haagen Dazs* out of her hand. Popping the top, he dug in, creating the perfect pink curl on the spoon. Presenting it to her, he offered her the first bite. She accepted without hesitation, and hand cupping his forearm, hummed in bliss as strawberry flavored perfection hit her taste buds. Watching her eat, Ivar fed himself from the same spoon. Such an intimate gesture. One Sasha wasn't sure how to handle. He was a stranger, but...she frowned. Weird, but for some reason, he didn't feel like one. He felt familiar and safe. Good in a way she didn't understand and couldn't explain. As though, she'd known him all her life.

Ivar fed her another spoonful. She moaned in culinary delight.

His lips twitched as he eyed the table across the room. "What's with all the bats?"

Licking ice cream off her lip, Sasha followed his line of sight. Her gaze landed on her work station. Shoved up against the far wall, the large table doubling as her desk bowed beneath open text books, piles of maps, her laptop and...oh, yeah. A few bats—three full endoskeletons to be exact—mounted on wooden supports. "Research. My latest project."

Twirling the spoon in his hand, he raised a brow. "What kind?"

Passionate about her field of study, she didn't mind his curiosity. Or shrug off his interest. She loved talking about her job. "I'm an ecologist with the Department of Fish and Wildlife. I work as a wildlife conservationist. Right now, I'm tracking bats, trying to nail down numbers...animal population, breeding grounds, the effect of environmental erosion on different bat species nesting in the state."

"Important work," he said, taking another bite.

An understatement. Huge in so many ways. Particularly since bats affected the agricultural industry, keeping insect populations in check for farmers. All of which impacted the economy. Strange, sure, but true nonetheless. The domino effect came into play with the environment involved. Fewer bats equaled more pests, and that in turn, diminished crop count, the amount of food that made it onto store shelves and people's tables.

Direct correlation. Big impact.

"Difficult work, but I'm making headway," Sasha said with a shrug. "I landed some important funding this week...a couple of big companies have agreed to help pay for the project. Pretty significant. One of my goals is to bring everyone together over the issue. Conservation needs to be a community effort...individuals, corporations and big government all working together to safeguard the environment."

"You're trying to change the world."

"One bat at a time."

"Jesus, Sasha," he murmured, awe in his voice. "You're amazing...just fucking incredible."

The compliment sank deep, making her chest go tight. He meant it. Every single word. His tone, the look in his eyes, didn't lie. He respected what she was trying to do and...oh mercy. She was in trouble. So much for her wham, bam, thank you man attitude. Ivar was ruining her get-out-quick-in-the-morning mentality by being so freaking nice. Which meant she should kick him out...right now. Before things got serious and the night went to hell in a hand-basket. But as she held his gaze—heart pounding, admiration and need for him rising—Sasha committed the cardinal sin of one night stands. She whispered his name, and stepping away from smart, leaned in to kiss him stupid instead.

5

F laked out on the couch in the smallest living room he'd ever seen, Ivar watched Sasha sleep. Eyes closed, tucked up against his side, her chest rose and fell in a steady rhythm. His throat went tight as he studied her face. Precious kitten. So fragile in his arms. So trusting in his presence. Such a gift to his battle-hardened senses. More than he'd expected—or deserved. Fate, though, worked in mysterious ways, ensuring he collided with Sasha when he needed her most. In the space of a few hours, she'd done what no one else ever had and lifted the heaviness inside his heart. Banished the shadows too, helping him forget his despair...if only for a little while.

Strange in every way that counted.

He didn't do emotion. Not in the traditional sense anyway. Closed off from the world, he'd thought himself immune, far removed from matters of the heart. With her, though, he couldn't stem the tide of tenderness. She touched him in ways he didn't understand. He enjoyed her wit. Liked her feistiness and that she stood her ground. Whenever he pushed, she shoved back, putting him in his place, refusing to tolerate disrespect, making him aware he didn't want to show her any. Another revelation. One of many firsts tonight. Hell, he held a whole mitt-full at the moment, all the novel things she made him feel. The most startling one still surprised him. Gratefulness. He was so damned thankful she'd invited him in, allowed him into her home, into her arms and body, treating him like a normal male.

Him...a male most women avoided like the plague.

To be expected. He wasn't anyone's idea of a nice guy. His track record spoke volumes. History and circumstance had shaped him, dictating the path, honing his skills, making him into who he needed to be in order to survive. But here...right now, with her in his arms...Ivar wanted to be something else. Something more. A better male even though he knew it would come back to bite him. The certainty of it made him cringe. Yet even as he acknowledged what must be done, Ivar refused to do it. He couldn't kill her to cover his tracks. Couldn't do what he'd done to so many others—use his magic to drain her energy, the essence of her life-force—and live with himself afterward. His conscience, long quiet, but obviously alive, wouldn't let him.

Not after all she'd given him tonight.

Trailing his fingers over her jaw, he changed course to caress the curve of her cheek. Her eyelashes flickered, but she didn't wake. Exhausted from his loving, Sasha remained deep in slumber, recovering from his possession, all the pleasure he'd lavished on her in the wee hours. Every ounce he'd taken too. But it was over now and...

A pang echoed behind his breastbone.

The heaviness returned, making his chest ache. Ivar sighed, and caressing Sasha one last time, slid his arms from around her. Time to go. He couldn't stay. The sun was almost up. Ten minutes tops, and dawn would arrive, leaving him vulnerable. At the mercy of deadly ultra-violet rays. Sasha wouldn't understand the weakness that kept him inside during the day. Nor did he plan on sticking around to explain it. The less she knew about his lineage—and Dragonkind—the safer she would be, so...yeah. Enough with the sap routine. Mourning the end of the night, and the loss of her, wasn't his style.

Hit hard. Leave fast. His motto, and exactly the way he liked to operate.

Which meant he needed to put his ass in gear— get up, grab his clothes, and head for the door. Right now. Before she woke up and waylaid him. Before the sun crested the horizon. Before he got trapped inside with a female he wasn't sure he wanted to leave. But as he disengaged without waking her and rolled free, Ivar paused. Bare feet planted next to the couch, he frowned, wondering if he should mind-scrub her before he left. He pursed his lips. Probably.

Adjusting her memory of the night would ensure a number of things—his safety along with hers...Drag-onkind's continued anonymity in the human world. A win-win for everyone, and yet even knowing it was necessary, he didn't want to invade her mind but...

"Fucking hell," he muttered in resignation.

He needed to take her memory of him. No other option existed. Not if he wanted to get away scot-free. Hitting one knee, he knelt alongside her. Gaze riveted to her face, Ivar reached out and cupped the side of her neck. Soft skin caressed his fingertips, making his heart thump and his conscience squawk.

"I'm sorry, Sasha. Forgive me, kitten."

The sound of his voice made her shift on the couch.

A furrow between her brows, still fast asleep, she turned toward him. Regret punched through. Ivar shut it down, and refusing to turn away, slipped his other hand between her and the seat cushions. Fingers spread wide, he palmed her lower back, then dipped his head, and pressed his cheek to hers. She murmured his name. He whispered back, telling her it was all right as the Meridian hummed, opening the cosmic connection, allowing him to link into her life-force. Unable to resist, he drank in the way of his kind, drawing nourishing energy from her into his core. Hunger surged, clawing past reason as his dragon half rose. Magic whiplashed, surging through his veins and...oh God. She tasted good. So damned *good*. Better than any female he'd ever—

A snarl broke free, bubbling up his throat.

Sasha moaned in answer. With a quick shift, she buried her hands in his hair. Sensation spiked. The current amplified, immobilizing him as she connected to the Meridian through him. The powerful force that fed Dragonkind flexed. Energy detonated like a bomb, blasting him with cosmic debris. Pain burned beneath the surface of his skin. Heart throbbing, Ivar tried to break free. To push her away and sever the connection. Sasha tightened her grip, and turning the tables, used the Meridian against him, subduing his dragon half. Paralyzed now, unable to let go, his vision tunneled, then flickered, flaring bright, blinking off, spinning him around the lip of sensory overload.

His mind fogged, then went sideways inside his head. The mental slosh slowed his reaction as air rushed from his lungs, cutting off his oxygen supply. Deprivation set in, triggering his gag reflex. His stomach dipped. Bile washed into his mouth. Ignoring the awful taste, Ivar fought physical lockdown, struggling to disengage without hurting her, but...sweet Jesus. She was taking too much. Was draining his core energy while obliterating his ability to fight back. Something he needed to change. Faster than fast. Otherwise, she would kill him...in her fucking sleep.

Gritting his teeth, Ivar forced his muscles to unlock. Pain lashed him again. He kept going, fighting to break her hold on him. Non-contact. A serious amount of separation. It was the only way to combat the energy rush and ensure his survival. Body straining, shaking like a drug addict in withdrawal, he wrenched his hands from her skin. The current downgraded, then snapped, freeing him from the magical tether.

Sasha grumbled in protest.

Ivar didn't care. Breathing like a wounded race horse, he shoved away from the couch and backpedaled. He slammed into the armchair. Wooded legs skittered across the floor as he tripped over his own feet, careened into the kitchen, and scrambled toward the door. He didn't look back. Didn't stop for his clothes. Or search for his boots. Only one thing mattered. Freedom. He needed to get the hell away from Sasha. Away from sensory overload. Away from the mind-torque of cosmic connection.

Away from the compulsion he felt to return to her.

Sick to his stomach, Ivar stumbled over the threshold. The door clicked behind him. Cold air slapped at him as he staggered across the porch. Off balance, he lost his footing and fell down the steps. Wooden stair treads hammered his back, scraping a bloody trail across his skin. He landed at the bottom with a bone-jarring thud, and with a grunt, struggled to his feet.

His knees buckled and...goddamn it. She'd sucked him dry. Now nothing was working right. His body had gone haywire, messing with his coordination, hampering vital function. God, he couldn't even see straight. Legs acting like wet noodles, he dragged himself across the yard, past the stupid Jeep, and onto the road.

Sharp stones cut into his bare soles.

Ivar barely noticed. So close. He was so close now. Less than one hundred yards away from the firehouse and the safety of home. All he needed to do was hold on a little longer.

Seeing double, Ivar hobbled toward 28 Walton Street. A trio of industrial-size garage doors came into view. Squinting, he focused on the ordinary entrance between the last two. Stumbling beneath the overhang, he reached for the knob. His hand slipped off cold steel. With a curse, he tried again and caught metal. A sharp twist. A quick shove, and the wooden panel opened wide. Ivar staggered inside, swung the door closed behind him, and collapsed on the concrete floor. Teeth chattering, he rolled belly-up, and swallowing the bad taste in his mouth, let his eyes drift shut, and...

Thank God. He was safe and...all right, not quite undamaged. But beggars couldn't be choosers. Alive, after all, was better than dead, so...yeah. Lesson learned. No more sex with the gorgeous blonde down the street. Memory of him intact or not, Sasha was now off limits. For all time. No way would he make the same mistake twice. Or give her another opportunity to link in and drain him dry.

～

Coming awake in a flurry of movement, Sasha popped upright on the sofa. Afghan slung over her shoulders, she bounced on the edge of the seat cushion, and flipping the hair out of her eyes, looked around. Sunlight streamed through the living room window, blinding her a moment before she surged to her feet. Her bare soles landed with a thump on the area rug. The solid sound echoed in the quiet. Stretching her arms overhead, Sasha hummed. Man, she felt amazing this morning. Supercharged. Positively electric as though she'd been plugged in overnight.

The strange buzz pricked the nape of her neck, then spread, washing over the tops of her shoulders. Her skin came alive in a wash of goose bumps. Shaking off the super-willy, she tossed aside the crocheted throw, stepped around the coffee table and—

Stubbed her toe on something.

Sasha glanced down, then blinked. A steel-toed boot, big, black as lethal looking as the man who owed it. Following the trail of clothing, she took in the jeans slung over the back of the armchair. Her gaze settled on the leather jacket beneath the denim, then ping-ponged to the heap of white cotton crumpled on the floor next to it. Her mouth tipped up at the corners. Ivar. He was still here...somewhere. She scanned the kitchen, taking in the bank of cabinets beyond the breakfast bar. Nope. Not there. Stepping toward the chair, she scooped his T-shirt off the hardwood and pressed it to her nose. His scent enveloped her, making her sigh and feel stupid at the same time.

Breathing him in was such a girly thing to do, but she couldn't help herself.

She liked the way he smelled—fresh and clean, all male with more than his fair share of the exotic. She hummed again. Yum. Oh, so good. Calvin Klein cologne had nothing on him. Sasha huffed. Another idiotic thought, but after the night he'd given her—and all the pleasure—she was entitled to a little sappiness. A truckload of satisfaction too. Maybe even another round, considering he'd stuck around 'til morning.

Jazzed by the possibility, Sasha tugged his shirt over her head. Soft cotton brushed the tops of her thighs as she made an abrupt turn and headed for the double-wide hallway connected to the living room. Her bedroom lay beyond, along with a pint-sized bathroom that boasted a deep claw-foot tub, fancy candles and expensive bath salts. A lover's playground. Not that she'd ever considered it that way before. But with Ivar in the mix, the space took on new dimension. Biting the inside of her lip, Sasha stifled a moan. Oh mercy, the possibilities. She could have so much fun with him, hot water and...heaven help her...scented oil.

Anticipation curled in the pit of her stomach.

Her heart picked up a beat, thumping hard as she stopped in the corridor outside the bathroom. The door stood ajar, the edge an inch away from the jamb. Sasha raised her hand, then hesitated, a little unsure. Should she knock or wait? Despite the intimacy they'd shared, she didn't know. Wasn't familiar enough with the male psyche to determine whether disturbing him constituted a breech in one night stand protocol. Hand hovering in mid-air, she debated a moment, then...

Ah, screw it. Forget right and wrong. He'd already broken the rules by staying. She rapped her knuckles against the wood.

No answer. She frowned. "Ivar?"

Nothing. Not a peep. No sound at all, making her

aware of the absolute stillness in the house. The deafening quiet too. Which was well...a touch eerie. Peaking around the jamb, Sasha pushed on the panel with her fingertips. Hinges whispered as the door swung wide. Big tub with the shower curtain pulled back. Stand alone sink with an antique mirror mounted above it. Colorful stained glass window aglow in sunlight. No Ivar in sight. Turning on her heel, she crossed the hall and entered her bedroom.

Empty. Nobody there either.

Doing a one-eighty, Sasha returned to the living room. Feet pitter-pattering on the hardwood floor, she scanned the space again. Weird. Clothes scattered hither and yon, but otherwise everything was in its place. Well, other than the chair. Shoved to one side, it pointed toward the front door. Her gaze narrowed on the entryway. Rug askew, door unlocked, and slightly ajar. Alarm skittered down her spine. Jogging past the peninsula, Sasha reached the door, pushed it all the way closed, and flipped the deadbolt.

"Crap," she whispered, realizing Ivar was gone.

Gone. Like a naked thief in the night.

Her brows collided. What the hell? He'd left without his clothes. Talk about strange and...jeez. Who did that kind of thing anyway, just took off without a word or a stitch on? Incomprehension slammed through her. The impact stunned her for a moment before concern slithered deep, and her imagination went wild. Had something terrible happened to Ivar? Had she slept through it? Had someone broken into the house and...oh God. Her heart shuddered, kicking the inside of her chest as she stepped into the kitchen. Reaching out, she snatched her cell phone off the countertop. The quick movement sent Ivar's sunglasses spinning into her purse. Ignoring both, she touched the screen and...

Froze, thumb poised above the keypad.

Calling the police probably wasn't the best idea. Not until she possessed all the facts. Forcing herself to think, Sasha glanced around and frowned. Odd, but as she took in the scene instinct rose, telling her to put the phone down. No cops necessary. There wasn't anything to report. Ivar was unhurt. How did she know? Sasha didn't have a clue. But as her heartbeat stabilized, the buzz in her veins settled into certainty. Sure, she might not know where he'd gone—or why he'd abandoned his clothes—but she knew...just *knew*...he was all right. Which meant...

The one night stand was officially over.

The realization tightened her throat. Sasha swallowed hard and buried her reaction beneath a pile of pragmatism. Waking up alone was for the best. Yup. No doubt. The night was over. Completely done. Finish the chapter and close the book. She'd gotten what she wanted. Generous to a fault, Ivar had given her all she needed so...right. End of story. But even as Sasha set her phone back on the counter and told herself to let it go, an errant thought drifted through her mind, making her wonder if she would ever see him again.

A NOTE FROM THE AUTHOR

Thank you for taking the time to read Fury of a Highland Dragon. If you enjoyed it, please help others find my books so they can enjoy them too.

Recommend it: Please help other readers find this book by recommending it to friends, readers' groups, and discussion boards.

Review it: Let other readers know what you liked or didn't like about Fury of a Highland Dragon.

Lend it: This e-book is lending-enabled, so feel free to share it with your friends. Sign up for my newsletter to receive new release information and other freebies. You can follow me on Facebook or on Twitter under @coreenecallahan.

Book updates can be found at www.CoreeneCallahan.com

Thanks again for taking the time to read my books!

ALSO BY COREENE CALLAHAN

ABOUT THE AUTHOR

 Coreene Callahan is the bestselling author of the Dragonfury Novels and Circle of Seven Series, in which she combines her love of romance and adventure with her passion for history. After graduating with honors in psychology and taking a detour to work in interior design, Coreene finally returned to her first love: writing. Her debut novel, *Fury of Fire* was a finalist in the New Jersey Romance Writers Golden Leaf Contest in two categories: Best First Book and Best Paranormal. She lives in Canada with her family, a spirited Anatolian Shepard, and her wild imaginary world.

www.ingramcontent.com/pod-product-compliance
Lightning Source LLC
Chambersburg PA
CBHW011523100726
47899CB00010BD/3465